WE NEED TO TURN THE MAGIC ON.
WE NEED TO SAVE THE DAY.
COME ON!

Hi, I'm Tom, welcome to Treetopolis. This is a magical world in an old tree at the end of my garden. Let me show you around, and you can meet all of my friends!

But first we need to do the **moves** that turn our **magic** powers on. Are you ready?

TREE FU GO!

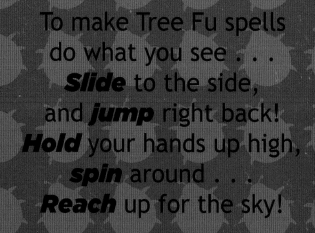

To make Tree Fu spells
do what you see . . .
Slide to the side,
and **jump** right back!
Hold your hands up high,
spin around . . .
Reach up for the sky!

Look, the
sapstone in my
belt is **glowing**!
Moving turned our
magic on. Let's
get going . . .

Here's my best friend Twigs!
He's an Acorn Sprite who can
do Tree Fu magic. Twigs is
really silly, funny and full
of brilliant energy.
We love playing, taking
turns leafboarding and
going on amazing
adventures together.
He's so much fun!

Twigs' favourite game is called Squizzle, where teams throw a spinning seed pod – called a Squizzle – trying to hit the three Wingseed goals. It's great fun! Down there is the Squizzle pitch.

Treetopolis is a busy place – there's always lots going on. This is where the Treelings live, alongside all kinds of creatures, from beetles and butterflies to woodlice and ladybirds.

Here is Treetop Castle
where the Sprites live.
The twisty-turny streets lead up
to the courtyard and Treetog's Tower
and Spell School at the very top.
Lots of amazing and fun events happen here!

Now let's find out more about
the magic. It's time to visit Treetog
in her tower. She is very clever
and everyone in Treetopolis can
learn from her. She's the
Tree Fu Master!

Look, here's Treetog's library! It's filled with books about everything you can think of, and there are many magical objects, too.

In Treetog's Tower and courtyard is Spell School, where Treetog teaches the Sprites all about Tree Fu magic. The sapstones in our belts help us make amazing magic with movements.

It's important to get the moves just right to make the magic work properly – practice makes perfect!

Twigs and I can do loads of brilliant things with Tree Fu magic, but sometimes on our adventures it's not strong enough to help us or to save our friends. That's when I need your help to make **BIG WORLD MAGIC**, which is the most powerful type of Tree Fu magic in all of Treetopolis.

When you do the Tree Fu moves with me, you make magic. Saying the spell words and pushing your hands forwards sends the magic to me, and makes a super-powerful spell to help me save the day! So you're a Tree Fu hero, too!

This is the Branch Ranch, where Ariela lives. She might be a pretty butterfly, but she's not afraid to get her hands dirty! Which is just as well, because around here there's always crops to plant or creatures to feed.

And here's one of those creatures now. This is Teabiscuit, a beetle who lives on the farm. He's huge and can be a bit of a handful at times, but luckily Ariela knows how to handle him!

Squirmtum is a woodlouse and is the biggest of my Treetopolis buddies. He likes to think he's super-tough, but he can actually be quite a scaredy cat and is sometimes even afraid of his own shadow!

There are caverns,
deep beneath Treetopolis,
where Squirmtum mines for magic sap.
It is ever so dark down there,
but a firefly called Flicker lives in
his helmet and lights the way.

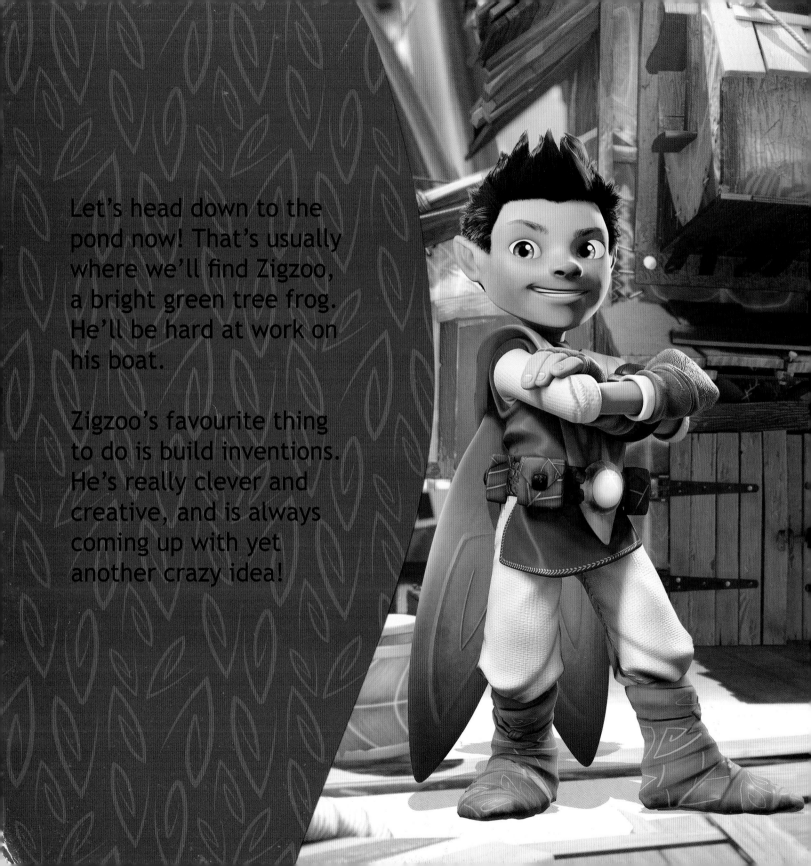

Let's head down to the pond now! That's usually where we'll find Zigzoo, a bright green tree frog. He'll be hard at work on his boat.

Zigzoo's favourite thing to do is build inventions. He's really clever and creative, and is always coming up with yet another crazy idea!

This overgrown canyon
is Rickety McGlum's garden.
It's often foggy and dark down
here, but there's nothing to
be afraid of, I promise!

Rickety is a spider, and for a long time everyone thought he was really scary. But he's not, he's actually very warm and wise! And now we have a new place in Treetopolis to explore . . .

Look, over there are Stink and Puffy, the Mushas. They are brother and sister and their favourite thing to do is make mischief in Treetopolis . . .

But with your help and **BIG WORLD MAGIC**,
we can stop them and save the day!
All you need to do is make the magic moves
with me and you can be a Tree Fu hero,
too! Keep practising those moves!

TREE FU GO!

Thanks for helping me in Treetopolis, see you soon for another adventure. Bye for now!

TREE FU TOM:
TREE FU GO!
A BANTAM BOOK
978 0 857 51160 7

Published in Great Britain
by Bantam, an imprint of Random House
Children's Publishers UK
A Random House Group Company.

This edition published 2013

1 3 5 7 9 10 8 6 4 2

Tree Fu Tom created by Daniel Bays.
TREE FU TOM word and device marks are trade marks of the British Broadcasting
Corporation and FremantleMedia Enterprises and are used under licence. TREE FU TOM
device marks © BBC and FremantleMedia Enterprises MMX. The "BBC" word mark and
logo are trade marks of the British Broadcasting Corporation and are used under licence.
BBC Logo © BBC 2012. Licensed by FremantleMedia Enterprises.

 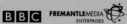

Bantam Books are published by Random House Children's Publishers UK,
61-63 Uxbridge Road, London W5 5SA

www.randomhousechildrens.co.uk

Addresses for companies within The Random House Group Limited can be found at:
www.randomhouse.co.uk/offices.htm

THE RANDOM HOUSE GROUP Limited Reg. No. 954009

A CIP catalogue record for this book is available
from the British Library

Printed in China

The Random House Group Limited supports the Forest Stewardship Council® (FSC®), the leading international
forest certification organization. Our books carrying the FSC label are printed on FSC®-certified paper.
FSC is the only forest certification scheme endorsed by the leading environmental organizations, including Greenpeace.
Our paper procurement policy can be found at www.randomhouse.co.uk/environment